Ms. Frizzle's Adventures
IMPERIAL CHINA

by JOANNA COLE
illustrated by BRUCE DEGEN

SCHOLASTIC INC.

NEW YORK TORONTO LONDON AUCKLAND SYDNEY
MEXICO CITY NEW DELHI HONG KONG BUENOS AIRES

For information regarding permission,
write to Scholastic Inc., Attention: Permissions
Department, 557 Broadway, New York, NY 10012.
ISBN-13: 978-0-590-10823-2 • ISBN-10: 0-590-10823-9 • Text
copyright © 2005 by Joanna Cole. Illustrations copyright © 2005 by
Bruce Degen. All rights reserved. Published by Scholastic Inc. SCHOLASTIC,
THE MAGIC SCHOOL BUS, MS. FRIZZLE'S ADVENTURES, and associated logos are
trademarks and/or registered trademarks of Scholastic Inc.
12 11 10 9 8 7 6 5 4 3 2   8 9 10 11 12 13/0   Printed in the U.S.A. 08
First Scholastic trade paperback printing, January 2008
The text type was set in 15-point Gill Sans. The illustrator
used brush and ink, pen, and gouache in the artwork.
The author and artist thank Valerie Hansen, Professor
of History at Yale University for her many thoughtful
comments on the manuscript and illustrations;
Kang-i Sun Chang, Professor of Chinese Literature
at Yale University, for her help in finding a suitable
Song dynasty poem; Matthew Towns for his
translation of Su Shi's poem; James Stepanek for
his calligraphy; Phoebe Yeh and Marion Yeh for
their generous comments and insight
from the Chinese American perspective;
and, as always, our heartfelt appreciation
to our editors, Kristin Earhart and Craig
Walker, for their encouragement,
suggestions, and overall wisdom.

Ms. Frizzle's Adventures
IMPERIAL CHINA

To my granddaughter, Annabelle.
May good fortune always
follow her.
—J.C.

To the memory of
Hymie and Mae
and the hot Chinese mustard.
—B.D.

It was the end of the school day,
and I, Ms. Frizzle, was on the move.
Wanda, one of my favorite students,
had invited me to spend
Chinese New Year's Eve with her family.
Wasn't that nice of her?

DRAGON KITE

WHERE IS CHINA? CHINA IS IN ASIA

NORTH AMERICA

EUROPE

ASIA

AFRICA

CHINA

SOUTH AMERICA

AUSTRALIA

N W E S

FISH KITE

MAKING KITES

Bamboo Strips

PAPER

BUTTERFLY KITE

WHEN IS CHINESE NEW YEAR?

In Western countries,
New Year's Day always falls
on January 1.

In China, the holiday
comes at a different
time each year.
It can be at the end of
January, or in February.

AND IT LASTS FOR
15 WHOLE DAYS!

JANUARY

S	M	Tu	W	Th	F	Sa
	1	2	3	4	5	6
7	8	9	10	11	12	13
14	15	16	17	18	19	20
21	22	23	24	25	26	27
28	29	30	31			

FEBRUARY

S	M	Tu	W	Th	F	Sa
				1	2	3
4	5	6	7	8	9	10
11	12	13	14	15	16	17
18	19	20	21	22	23	24
25	26	27	28			

That evening, I went to meet Wanda's family. Before dinner, we strolled around Chinatown, taking in the holiday sights.

The New Year's festival was exciting.
A cloth dragon came winding down the street.
Men were under the dragon, making it dance.
Wanda has always been an adventurous girl,
but even I was surprised by what she did next.

YOU CAN'T GO UNDER THERE—YOU'LL MISS DINNER!

I CAN'T GO UNDER HERE—I'LL MISS KUNG FU!

WHAT IT MEANS IN CHINA

The Dragon means good luck and power. It was a symbol of the Emperor in ancient China.

Dragon painting

Dragon pottery

Dragon robe

Wanda ducked under the dragon.
Henry followed her, and naturally,
Arnold was eager to join them.
I, Ms. Frizzle, went too.
After all, someone had to make sure
they didn't get too far from home.

IT'S COOL, ARNIE.
YOU CAN TAKE A
MAKEUP CLASS.

We were under the dragon
for a long time.

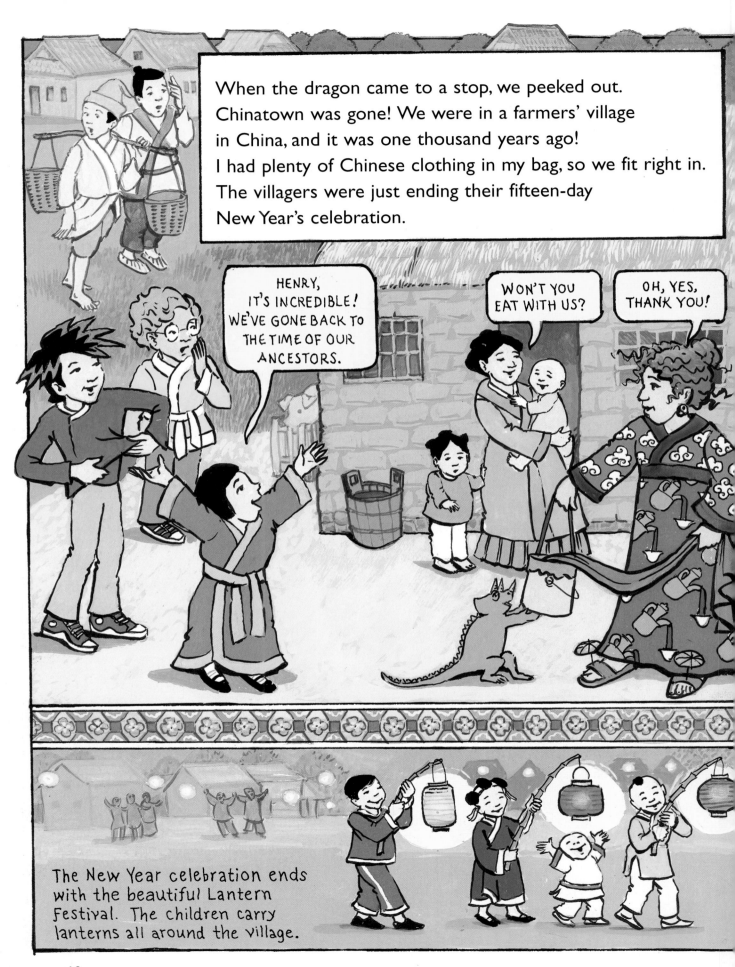

When the dragon came to a stop, we peeked out. Chinatown was gone! We were in a farmers' village in China, and it was one thousand years ago! I had plenty of Chinese clothing in my bag, so we fit right in. The villagers were just ending their fifteen-day New Year's celebration.

The New Year celebration ends with the beautiful Lantern Festival. The children carry lanterns all around the village.

Even though we were complete strangers, the farmers shared their food with us and invited us to stay overnight.

Farmers' families had to sell lots of rice to earn enough money to pay their taxes. When the rice crop was small, the governor was supposed to make the taxes lower, but this year he wanted to keep the same high taxes.

WE CAN'T PAY OUR TAXES.

THE EMPEROR MIGHT HELP US. EVERYONE KNOWS HE IS KIND.

BUT THE EMPEROR IS FAR AWAY.

PAY ATTENTION TO THIS WORD

When you pay TAXES, you give some of what you earn to the government.

WE USE YOUR MONEY FOR ROADS, CANALS, ARMIES...

...PALACES, JEWELS, FANCY CLOTHES FOR THE GOVERNOR.

COLLECT THE TAXES NOW!

Tax collector | Farmer | Tax collector | THE GOVERNOR

The great Yangtze River flowed past the farm.
That gave Wanda an idea.
"Let's go talk to the Emperor about this," she said.
I, Ms. Frizzle, did not hesitate.
Right then and there, I booked us passage
on a river barge headed for the palace.

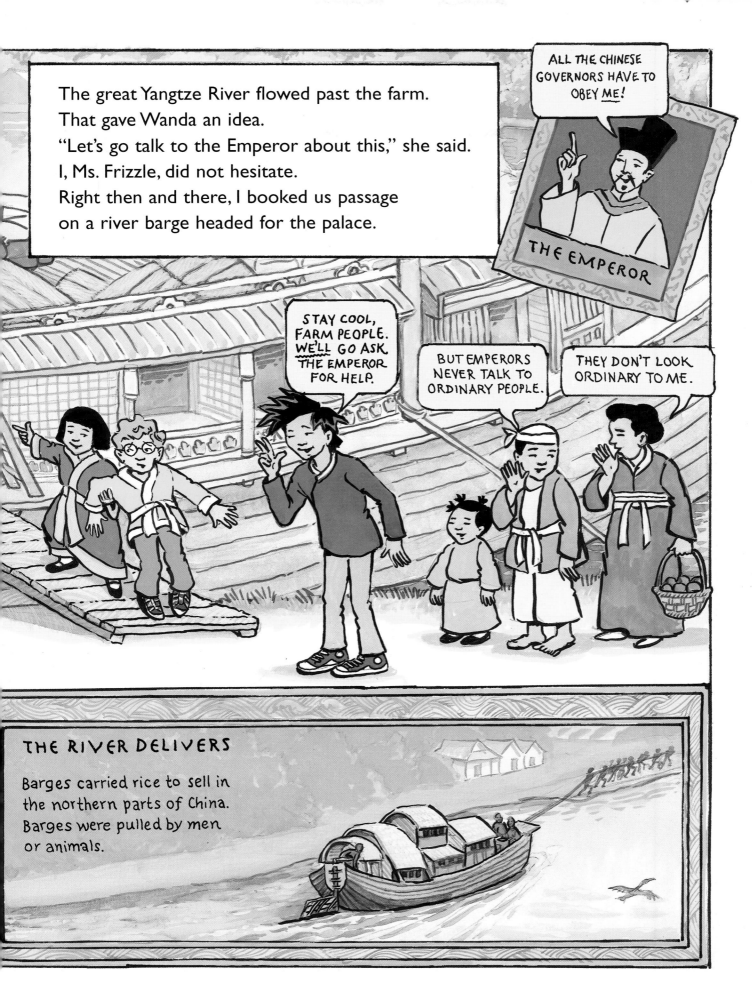

THE RIVER DELIVERS

Barges carried rice to sell in the northern parts of China. Barges were pulled by men or animals.

We cruised down the river, eating, drinking tea,
and sleeping on board.
We stopped along the way to pick up more loads of rice.
Finally, we came to the Grand Canal, which
would take us north to the Emperor.
There, a new traveler came aboard.

FIRST BREWED IN CHINA

TEA ~ 2,300 Years ago
People around the world drink tea more than any other beverage except water.

1. Tips of tea bushes are picked.

2. Tea leaves are dried and prepared.

3. Tea is brewed with hot water in teapots.

4. In ancient China tea was often sipped from bowls instead of cups.

Our new passenger was a poet named Su Shi.
As soon as he came on the boat,
he started to write a poem.
I, Ms. Frizzle, was delighted!
I even copied it in English for my class's China studies.

chinese writing reads from top to bottom, and from right to left.

橫看成嶺側成峰
遠近高低各不同
不識廬山真面目
只緣身在此山中

POEM IN ENGLISH
From the side,
    a whole range,
From the end,
    a single peak.
Far, near, high, low,
    no two parts alike.
Why can't I tell the
    true shape
        of Mt. Lu?
Because I myself
    am in the mountain.

CHINESE WRITING

Chinese writers use symbols called "characters." Each one stands for a word. Combining two characters can make another word.

火山

Fire   + Mountain = Volcano

There were special supplies for writing and drawing in ancient China:

Inkstick   Inkstone   Water Jar   Bamboo Brushes

Inkstick
Well
Inkstone

To make Chinese ink, rub an inkstick with water on an inkstone until the ink in the well is as dark as you wish.

In his travels, the poet had learned that the Emperor would be leaving the capital soon. There were many rich palaces in China, and the Emperor lived in them, one after another. Oh, dear! We had to get to the capital fast, or we would miss the Emperor!

THE EMPEROR WILL GO AWAY VERY SOON.

WON'T THIS BOAT GO FASTER?

I DON'T THINK SO...

FIRST INVENTED IN CHINA

RUDDER
for steering a boat
2,000 years ago

Rudder

COMPASS
for finding direction
more than 1,000 years ago

Magnetized needle
Float
Bowl of water

Simple Mariner's Compass

We found ourselves in a busy town, and there was so much to see! We were buying some souvenirs, when we were invited to learn how silk is made. Somehow, we just couldn't say no.

COME WITH US.

WE NEED WORKERS.

FIRST INVENTED IN CHINA

PAPER
about 2,100 years ago
Paper was made by grinding mulberry bark into pulp and spreading it on a screen to dry into sheets.

PAPER MONEY
about 1,000 years ago
Before paper money, Chinese coins were made of bronze. They had square holes for stringing.

THIS MONEY IS TOO HEAVY!

TRY SOME OF THIS!

At the factory, we started learning
the silk trade right away.
Making silk is hard work.
Now, I usually do not mind hard work,
but we were on a mission.
We had to get to the capital city and
talk to the Emperor!

MULBERRY TREES

WE HAVE TO GET AWAY!

IT WON'T BE EASY.

HOW TO MAKE SILK

1. Feed silkworms. (They eat only mulberry leaves.)

2. Let worms spin cocoons out of silk.

ACTUAL SIZE

3. Dip cocoons in hot water to dissolve sticky stuff.

THIS ISN'T COOL.

IT'S HOT!

When we woke up,
we had gone too far.
We had missed the capital.
We had come all the way
to the Great Wall of China!
The wall was built to keep
out invaders, and at that
very moment, an invading
army was trying to get in.

THE GREAT WALL:
1,000 YEARS AGO
At first it was made of
mounds of earth with spaces
in between. Sometimes it fell
down and had to be rebuilt.

THE GREAT WALL:
TODAY
It finally became a stone wall
more than 4,160 miles long.
It is the largest human-made
structure on Earth.

IT TOOK THOUSANDS OF YEARS...

...AND MILLIONS OF WORKERS...

...TO BUILD THIS WALL.

Warriors from lands to the north were fighting on horseback. They wanted to conquer and rule China. The Chinese soldiers were fighting back from the top of the dirt wall.

TAKE THAT!

AARRGGHH!

FIRST INVENTED IN CHINA

CROSSBOW
2,300 years ago

A crossbow was faster and more powerful than an ordinary bow and arrow.

GUNPOWDER
1,200 years ago

Arrows could now carry gunpowder charges.

STEEL
1,500 years ago

Swords could be made of steel.

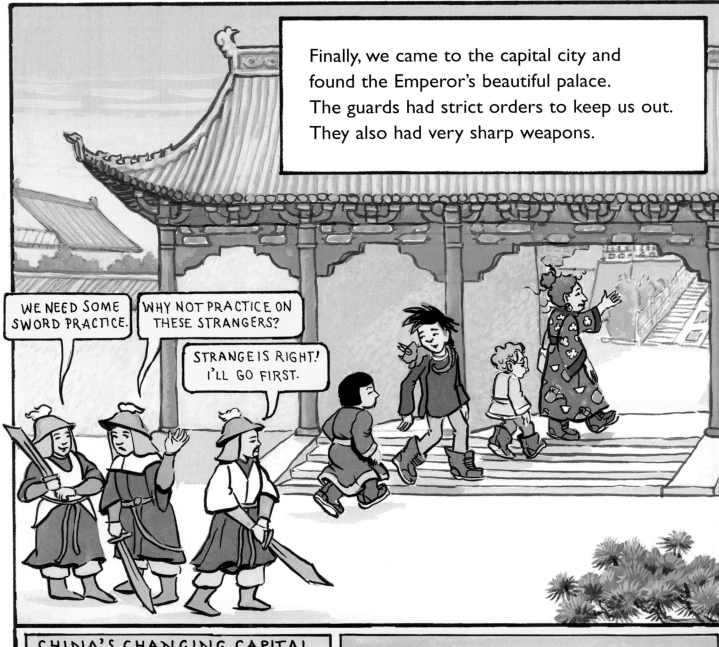

Finally, we came to the capital city and found the Emperor's beautiful palace. The guards had strict orders to keep us out. They also had very sharp weapons.

WE NEED SOME SWORD PRACTICE.

WHY NOT PRACTICE ON THESE STRANGERS?

STRANGE IS RIGHT! I'LL GO FIRST.

CHINA'S CHANGING CAPITAL

China's capital has moved many times. In the 11th century it was Kaifeng.

Today the capital is Beijing. This city has been the capital several times over thousands of years.

In Beijing you can still visit the ancient Emperor's palace in a walled area called the Forbidden City.

THE FORBIDDEN CITY

It looked like they were going to
use their swords on us.
Fortunately, they changed their minds.
We just had to get inside the palace and
find the Emperor.

We entered the palace, passing beautiful furniture, jade sculptures, and porcelain vases. Treasures were all around us, but the person we were looking for was nowhere to be seen. Was he even in the palace?
We hoped we weren't too late!

UH-OH. HERE COMES ANOTHER GUARD!

BE COOL, ARNIE. I DON'T THINK HE SEES US.

FIRST INVENTED IN CHINA

PORCELAIN
about 1,500 years ago
Pottery is clay fired in an oven.
Porcelain is a very, very fine quality of pottery that is used to make vases and dishes.
Because porcelain was first invented in China, English-speaking people call all dishes "china."

EARTHQUAKE DETECTOR
more than 1,800 years ago
When the earth shakes, metal balls fall into the mouths of the toads, and show the direction and strength of the quake.

Then Wanda, who was always running ahead, looked in a doorway and made a grand discovery. Thank goodness—the Emperor of China was still at home!

LOOK, MS. FRIZZLE! I FOUND HIM!

COOL OUTFIT, EMP.!

CAN WE GET HIS AUTOGRAPH?

BE RESPECTFUL, KIDS.

JADE CARVING
5,000 years ago
Jade is a rare stone that is carved into jewelry and statues.

PIN   DISC   JAR

WHAT IT MEANS IN CHINA

IMPERIAL YELLOW
The Emperor's robes were a special shade of yellow. Nobody but the Emperor was allowed to wear that color.

The Emperor was not only the ruler of a great country, he was a talented artist, too.
He turned from his painting and asked what we wanted.
Wanda told him all about the farmers' village, the small rice crop, and the unfair taxes.
I, Ms. Frizzle, was so proud of her!

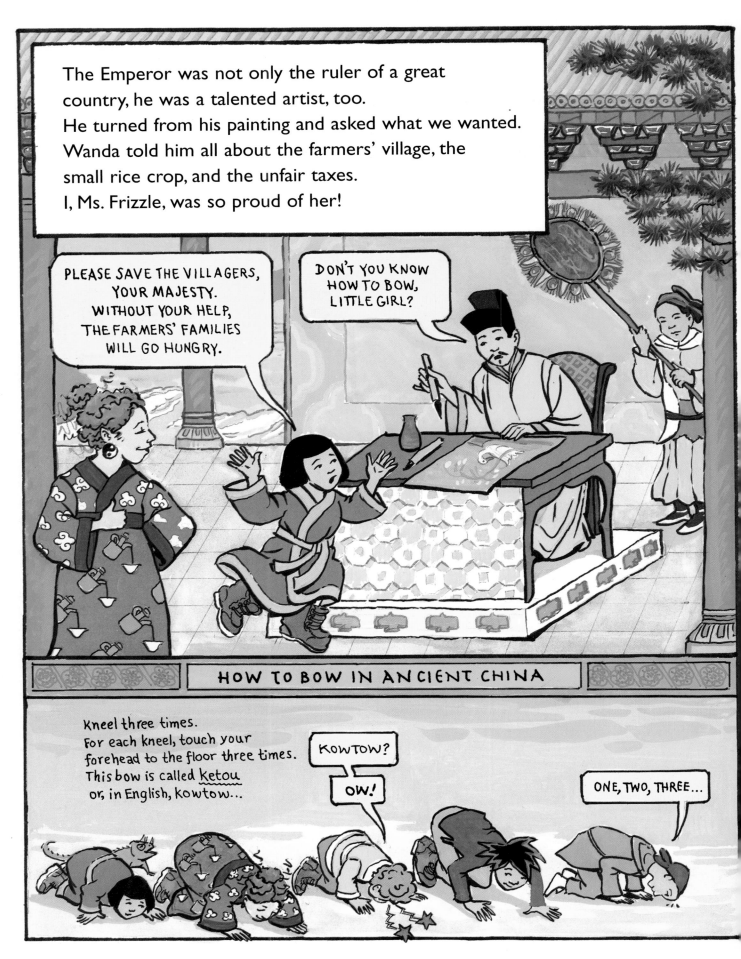

PLEASE SAVE THE VILLAGERS, YOUR MAJESTY. WITHOUT YOUR HELP, THE FARMERS' FAMILIES WILL GO HUNGRY.

DON'T YOU KNOW HOW TO BOW, LITTLE GIRL?

HOW TO BOW IN ANCIENT CHINA

Kneel three times. For each kneel, touch your forehead to the floor three times. This bow is called ketou or, in English, kowtow...

KOWTOW?

OW!

ONE, TWO, THREE...

The Emperor understood at once.
He announced that there would be no taxes
that year for farmers who had small rice crops!
He sent an official to inform the village's governor.

Now it was time to leave.

We knew we had to get home. Unfortunately, the guard was in our way. Fortunately, Arnold had some fast moves.

HAI-AH!

YIKES! HE KNOWS KUNG FU!

LOOK, MS. FRIZZLE! ARNOLD IS PRACTICING HIS KUNG FU!

HIS MOTHER WILL BE SO PLEASED.

QUICK! LET'S GET OUT OF HERE!

FIRST INVENTED IN CHINA

KUNG FU ~ Thousands of years ago
Kung fu is a kind of unarmed martial art.
UNARMED - without weapons
MARTIAL - fighting
ART - skill

WHAT IT MEANS IN CHINA

The lion is thought to guard against danger. Lion sculptures are often put outside a door. It is good luck to rub a paw as you go by.

Our luck continued.
Wanda came upon a handy door.
It was an amazing door.
In fact, it was the door to . . .

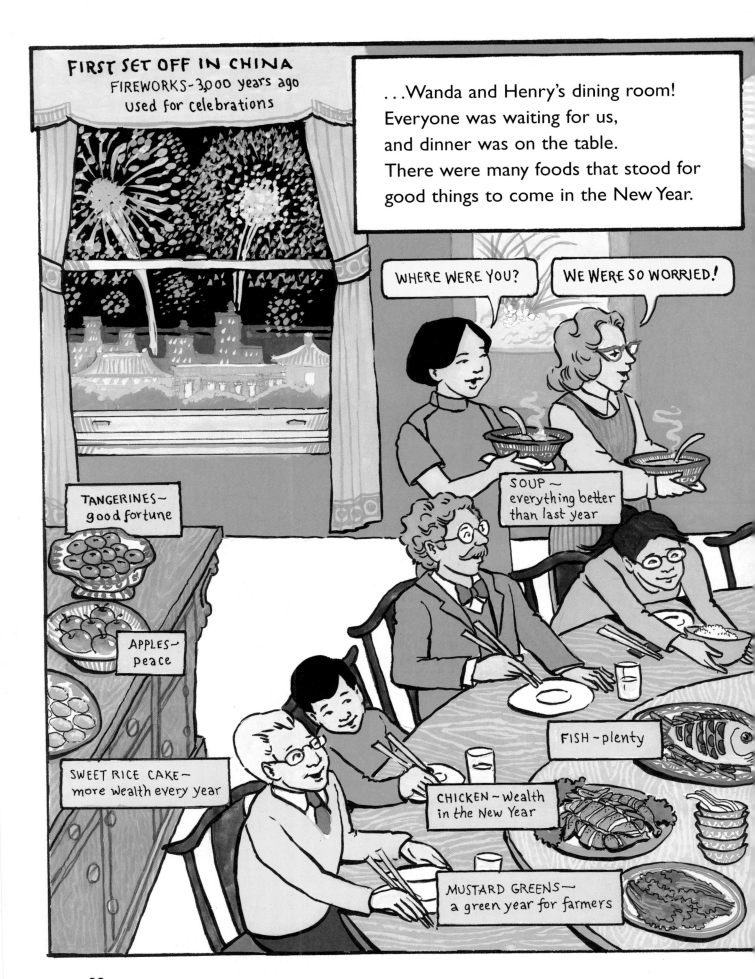

We had worked up quite an appetite. There's nothing like a delicious New Year's banquet to round off a lovely afternoon of sight-seeing!

CAUTION!

WE ARE V.S.P., AND WE SAY,
"THIS BOOK HAS ERRORS AND OMISSIONS!"

V.S.P. STANDS FOR VERY SMART PEOPLE.

I THINK IT STANDS FOR VERY SNOOTY PEOPLE.

We are **V**ery **S**mart **P**eople, and we found that lots of important facts about China were left out of this story. We also found many things that were not true. In fact, they were downright *ridiculous!*

First and foremost, Ms. Frizzle could not travel to China and be back in Walkerville in time for dinner. Such a trip takes many hours even in an airplane, and we do not think a paper dragon can go very fast at all.

This book suggests that Ms. Frizzle can go back in time, but we know that time travel is impossible. It is also impossible to fit all those clothes and boots into one small bag.

Many Chinese inventions were left out of this book; for instance: printing, movable type, the suspension bridge, matches, masts and sails for boats, cast iron, and many more. The author says it was because there was not enough space. You should read some other books about China to learn more.

This book does get some things right. There really was a poet named Su Shi, and he did write the poem in the book. But we know that it could not have been written on a river barge because the title of the poem is "Written on a Wall at West Forest Temple."

There also really was a kind emperor who was an artist. His name was Huizong, and the paintings hanging in the palace in this book are true reproductions of works by Emperor Huizong. But an emperor — even a very kind one — was an exalted, godlike person. He actually would not have talked to ordinary people.

We feel strongly that a book should not show kids running away from their parents — especially if they are accompanied by a teacher like Ms. Frizzle.

Last, but not least, Arnold really did scare the guard away so everyone could escape. And Ms. Frizzle really does know everything.